Rachel Isadora

I HEAR

Greenwillow Books, New York

Y PRE

Library of Congress Cataloging in Publication Data

Isadora, Rachel.
I hear.
Summary: A baby responds to all
the familiar things she hears.
1. Babies—Fiction.
2. Hearing—Fiction]
I. Title.
PZ7.I763Iah 1985   [E]   84-6103
ISBN 0-688-04061-6
ISBN 0-688-04062-4 (lib. bdg.)

For Gillian Heather

I hear a bird.
Chirp, chirp.

I hear the clock.
Tick tock.

I hear footsteps.
It's Mommy
and
Daddy.

I hear the kettle
whistle.
Time for breakfast.

I hear
the vacuum.
Vroom,
vroom.

I hear my cat.
Meow, meow.

I hear the ducks.
Quack, quack.

I hear an airplane.
I look up.

I hear music.
I dance.

I hear the rain.
Splish splash.

I hear
the dragon.
I roar.

I hear water.
Bathtime.

I hear a story.
I laugh.

I hear a lullaby.

Good night.